Harry Chance

Christmas 1983.

PUSHKIN THE POLAR BEAR

Pastelein

PUSHKIN THE POLAR BEAR

Simon Gaul
Illustrated by Hugh Casson

Simon Gaul

Hugh Casson

A Quartet/Visual Arts Book

A Quartet/Visual Arts Book

First published 1983
Quartet Books Limited
27/29 Goodge Street, London W1P 1FD

British Library Cataloguing in Publication Data
Gaul, Simon
    Pushkin the polar bear.
    I. Title   II. Casson, *Sir Hugh*
    823'.914[J]   PZ7

ISBN 0-7043-2416-4

SAGDOS - Printed in Italy

For Camilla and Paul, without forgetting Georgina

Polar Bears live at the North Pole. Pushkin lived with his mother and father at the South Pole, for wherever there is snow you can be sure there are Polar Bears.

Pushkin was a slightly chubby and happy Polar Bear. He had his friends who he played with in the snow, and went to school (even Polar Bears go to school).

One day, when all the other Polar Bears had gone home, he stayed out in the snow building a snowman. Suddenly something happened. The world stopped spinning for a split second. Pushkin was just about to put his blue hat on the snowman when he found himself whirled off into space. Higher and higher he

floated until the South Pole became a white dot miles below him. He felt very light, despite the fact that he was really a bit fat and usually felt quite heavy. The sky was dark, but the stars shone brightly, so close that he could almost touch them. It felt just like being carried by his mother, so it didn't frighten him. He enjoyed floating along. But his tummy started to rumble, and that told him it was long past tea-time. Soon he began to think he would like to go home. But he couldn't stop floating, so warmed by his fur he dozed off to sleep, dreaming of ice creams and other cold things to eat.

All of a sudden Pushkin woke up with a bang. His nose felt cold, as if it was buried in the ice creams he had dreamt about. His head hurt as well, which was strange because it had never hurt before.

He had landed face down in the snow with a big thud. Little stars were flying around his sore head. Although he did not know it, he had just become the first Polar Bear to fly through space from the South Pole to the North Pole. As he sat in the snow and looked around, he rubbed his head and wiped the cold snow from his nose.

'Must be home,' thought Pushkin, 'there's snow everywhere.'

Then he realized that he could not see anything familiar, except, of course, snow: no rocks or igloos, let alone any Eskimos. But he did see in the distance something that looked like the snowman he had been building. The trouble was that it seemed to be moving. It had a hat and a long scarf; but his snowmen didn't walk. Pushkin decided to ignore it and just go home. But as it got closer, it looked less like a snowman and more like a large Polar Bear. This puzzled Pushkin. No one he knew wore a hat and a coloured scarf – apart from snowmen, that is. He stood as tall as he could on tiptoe and sat down with a thud again. 'It really is another bear,' thought Pushkin, 'and a big one. How very strange.' He scratched his head for a moment and then trotted off in the direction of the hat and scarf.

'What are you doing here?' asked the bear in a growly voice. He was big, even bigger than Pushkin's father who was famously big.

'Uh, uhm, I could ask you the same question,' replied Pushkin, not cheekily, but because he wanted to know.

'I live here, that's what I'm doing here,' boomed the big bear.

'Well so do I, but I haven't seen you before. My name is Pushkin,' he said.

'My name is Digby and I haven't seen you before either,' said the bear, in a quieter voice.

Pushkin was bewildered. He had a sore head, his nose was still very cold. He couldn't see his home or any of his friends' homes. But his tummy continued to grumble and protest, which made him forget his confusion.

'Mr Digby,' said Pushkin politely, 'I think I'm lost and I'm awfully hungry'

'My name is Digby, not Mr Digby. I know just what you need.' Like a magician he untied his scarf to show four fish hidden in its folds.

'Come on, let's go and have some food. Then we can find out where you live.' Digby was a special bear, very old and wise and Polar Bears for miles around would come to ask his advice on all manner of things. He had been asleep when the world had stopped spinning, but he knew something strange had happened because he had been thrown out of bed. 'That might have something to do with Pushkin's being lost,' thought Digby.

He didn't live very far away, so together they set off home to cook the fish. Digby's home was a large cave, with a very small front door that Pushkin could walk through; but Digby had to crawl. Once inside, Pushkin saw a big fire and lots of blankets. All the walls were lined with books. They didn't look anything like the books he had seen at school. Digby cooked the supper, while Pushkin warmed his nose by the fire. He did not say a word; not only was his stomach painfully empty, but Digby had said they would talk after supper.

They feasted themselves on fish and icebergs of ice cream and after the last mouthful Pushkin stroked his stomach. 'Mr Digby – sorry Digby – will you help me to get home?' he asked.

Digby didn't reply. Instead he walked to a bookshelf and stretching as high as he could took down a large dusty book. Pushkin had never seen a book that size before; it was as big as a table and Digby nearly toppled under its weight.

'Ah, I haven't looked at this for so long, no need to any more.' Digby breathed the dust off it as he spoke. Finally, he laid the book down in front of Pushkin.

'What is it?' said Pushkin, still mystified.

'An atlas,' replied Digby.

'What's an atlas?' asked Pushkin, who had not seen one before. Young Polar Bears are never taught geography because they are much too adventurous and love to explore.

Digby didn't answer, he just opened the big book. Pushkin gazed at it in bewilderment. The map of the world looked like lots of bright colours all joined together.

'Now listen carefully Pushkin,' said Digby, 'this is a drawing of the world, where we live.'

'Why is it all different colours?' piped up Pushkin. 'Where I live it is all white.'

'Don't interrupt; there are many more places in the world than just where you live.' Digby thought hard; it was going to be very difficult to explain to Pushkin that he was thousands of miles from home.

'Well,' said Pushkin with his eyes wide open, 'will you show me where we are, please Digby?'

Digby pointed to the top of the book where it was white.

'Huh, so I live at the top of the world,' said Pushkin proudly.

'No Pushkin, you don't, you live here.' Digby pointed to the white at the bottom of the page.

Pushkin's mouth opened, but no noise came out. Digby explained as well as he could what had happened to Pushkin. When the old bear had finished, he put his arm round Pushkin. 'Don't worry, Pushkin, you can stay with me.'

'I don't want to be rude, Digby, but I must go home. If you say that we are at the top of the world and I live at the bottom, I still have to get home. Anyway my parents would miss me if I didn't,' said Pushkin firmly.

'Pushkin, do you know how far it is?' Digby's words were lost on Pushkin for his mind was made up. As much as he liked Digby he liked his home better.

'Digby, I believe I can get home,' said Pushkin, who was very brave. He paused and stood up, saying 'I got here didn't I?' Digby nodded his head.

'Will you please draw me a picture like that one, so I can take it with me?' asked Pushkin, pointing to the atlas. Again Digby nodded his head.

'I couldn't carry the atlas all the way home, despite the fact that it's all downhill,' announced Pushkin.

This time Digby shook his head slowly, knowing he could not teach Pushkin everything he needed to know about the world. Digby told Pushkin that every day the sun would rise on the left of the map and sink on the right if he was going in the correct direction. He marked a few cities on the map and told Pushkin to look out for Vienna, where a friend of his lived in the zoo. But he forgot to tell Pushkin what a zoo was. Pushkin was comforted by the thought that there must be Polar Bears all over the world.

The very next morning he waved goodbye to Digby, and set off on what he thought would be a long downhill walk home. Digby had cut his scarf in half and given a piece to Pushkin. There were, of course, two fish tied to it in case he got hungry.

He had never slept in the open before, but he soon got used to it. He ate the two fish very quickly, for he found that all that walking made him hungry. Food was scarce, but occasionally he came across a lake where he would stop and fish. He always ate and ate until he nearly burst. If there were any fish left over he tied them in his scarf for another day.

Soon the snow and ice became grey and slushy. He wouldn't have noticed at all, if his feet hadn't got warmer. He did not really know where he was, although he often looked at his map in a knowledgeable way.

In fact he was in Russia. He didn't think much of it because it looked as if it were deserted and the ground was a nasty greeny-brown colour. Besides, he hadn't seen any other Polar Bears. The days passed, and he felt lonely as he trudged on, always keeping the rising sun on his left.

The weather became warmer, and Pushkin was very tired, but all he thought about was getting home. Pushkin remembered what Digby had taught him, and hoped that he would soon find somewhere called Vienna. Many days and nights later he came across a sign that read 'Vienna 10 km'. He stared at it, for he was looking for 'Vienna' not 'Vienna 10 km', but he followed the sign, content with the thought that Vienna could not be far from 'Vienna 10 km'.

As he got closer to Vienna he began to feel afraid. He had never seen so many people and noisy machines before. Pushkin kept out of sight as much as he could but he still had the problem of finding the 'zoo', where Digby's friend lived. He was looking forward to seeing him, as he hadn't seen a Polar Bear for ages.

'There is a problem,' thought Pushkin. 'I don't know what a zoo looks like, so I don't know what I am looking for.' But the problem was soon solved. People in the street began shouting 'Polar Bear' and running away. He heard someone shout 'Call the zoo' and Pushkin began to relax, thinking to himself that a 'zoo' must be a home for Polar Bears. Still he could not understand why the people were afraid and running away. He wasn't going to harm anyone. Then he remembered that when he saw people at home he ran away from them. This was their home, so it must be obvious for them to run away from him.

Before he could think any more he heard a loud wailing noise getting closer and closer. It was the sound of a siren, on a large white truck, with 'Zoo' written on the side in big black letters. Pushkin began to have doubts about a zoo being a home for Polar Bears. Suddenly he felt a stinging in his side. One of the zoo-keepers had fired a drugged dart in him. He crumpled heavily to the ground.

When Pushkin woke up, many hours later, the first thing he saw was a large Polar Bear smiling at him.

'Where am I?' asked Pushkin, still feeling drowsy.

'You are in the zoo,' said the bear. 'Do you feel all right?'

'A bit sleepy. What happened?'

'They have just brought you here,' said the strange bear. 'You must be a friend of Digby's. That's his scarf you are wearing.'

'Ah,' said Pushkin, beginning to stir, 'so you are Digby's friend. What's your name? Digby said you would help me.'

'My name is Tovvy, short for Tovarich, which is Russian for friend. Tell me where you saw Digby and how you got here.'

So Pushkin began to tell his story while Tovvy sat quietly trying to think of a way to help him. He was amazed at Pushkin's story and his faith in his efforts to get home. Tovvy thought it was a miracle that he had got as far as Vienna. When Pushkin had finished, Tovvy told him his own story, of how he was captured many years ago, and brought to the zoo. He told Pushkin of the life he and Digby had known, when he was free. Unlike Digby, he remembered to tell Pushkin all about zoos.

'I don't like the sound of zoos,' said Pushkin. 'We have got to escape.'

'Nor do I, but I have lived here too long now and I am too old to try to get out. Anyway you have confused all the zoo-keepers; they thought you had run away

from here, but when they brought you here they discovered that you were not one of their bears after all, because you were not here in the first place. Do you understand?' asked Tovvy, himself a bit puzzled.

'I'm not sure. All I know is I have to get home.' Pushkin liked Tovvy, for he had a kind face and besides, he was a friend of Digby's.

When the zoo-keeper had thrown their fish into the cage that evening, they sat down. Pushkin thought sadly of the time that Digby had cooked supper. The fish were much nicer there.

During supper Tovvy explained to Pushkin a plan he had for escape.

'Tovvy, please come with me,' said Pushkin when Tovvy had finished talking.

'No, I'm too old now and Digby said I was to help you so it would be better if I stayed here.'

'Tovvy, don't you want to escape? Don't you want to go home? I'm sure Digby would love to see you again, or perhaps you would like to come home with me,' said Pushkin. It wasn't that he was afraid to try to make the journey home alone; it was just that he felt a Polar Bear's home was where the snow and ice were, not in a zoo. But Tovvy would not go.

In the dead of night, when all the other animals in the zoo were asleep, Tovvy helped Pushkin to climb the walls of their compound. Pushkin had two regrets as he climbed over the wall: he was sad that Tovvy was not coming with him and that he hadn't seen any of the other animals. To think that he had thought a zoo was a nice home for Polar Bears! Sad at leaving Tovvy, yet excited to be free,

Pushkin made his way through the dark streets of Vienna to the railway station. Tovvy had remembered to tell Pushkin what a train was and where to hide, and that as a small bear he could lose himself in a cattle-truck. Tovvy had explained that cattle looked like enormous dogs with thin legs.

Meanwhile, back in the zoo, Tovvy missed Pushkin. He hoped and prayed that his young friend would find the right train. It was a cattle-train which left for Sicily every week. From there the cattle were loaded on to a boat bound for Egypt. There hadn't been enough time to tell Pushkin all about Africa but Tovvy knew Pushkin was a clever bear, even if he was a bit too fat.

FRACHTBÜRO

Tovvy need not have worried. Pushkin found the right train at the station by following his nose. In the still night there was a strong smell which Pushkin guessed was coming from the cattle. The cows were astonished and made loud mooing noises when he got in. Not only had he not seen a cow before but the cows had not seen a Polar Bear either. There was enough room for everybody and the cows, like Pushkin, did not want an argument. The train spluttered into life soon after Pushkin had climbed into the truck. Having found a corner for himself Pushkin sat down and for the first time since he had left the North Pole and Digby, he cried. Not only for himself, but for Tovvy, his mother and father and all the animals in the zoo. He made a promise that if he ever got home again he would never stay out and play after his parents had told him not to.

But Pushkin was a brave bear so he stopped crying and feeling sorry for himself and settled down to sleep.

Pushkin was woken up by the hot sun beating down as the train made its way through the beautiful green countryside. He hadn't slept so well for ages. The cows ignored him and he dozed. The next time Pushkin woke up it was inky black outside and the train was beginning to slow down. 'We must be getting near the boat,' said Pushkin to himself. He had seen a few boats before when he was at home and he was thrilled to think he was going on one. Soon the cattle-trucks stopped and the slow process of loading them on to the boat began. Large cranes, illuminated by lights like little moons, lifted up the trucks. As his truck was moved from the train he thought, 'This is really exciting.'

By dawn, with the sun rising on the left of his map, Pushkin peered over the edge of the open truck to look at the harbour as the boat slowly chugged out of port. There weren't many people on shore, but he did see lots of other boats of all shapes and sizes and colours. The sea looked inviting to Pushkin for he found the early morning heat a little too strong.

'Well, I'm used to cold weather,' he muttered to himself. 'Everything seems to be going well. The sun has risen on the left of the map so I must be on course and there must be all sorts of fish in the sea.' Pushkin tried very hard to think of a way that he could fish, but the truck was a little too high on the deck and anyway he did not have a fishing line with him. The boat-journey was long, so Pushkin passed the time dreaming of Africa, wondering what it would be like and moaning about his stomach. Every day a large heap of greeny-brown stuff that looked like long bits of grass was thrown into the truck. The cows ate it very happily but Pushkin hated it. There was no taste or flavour to it and it was difficult to swallow, so he gave up eating it.

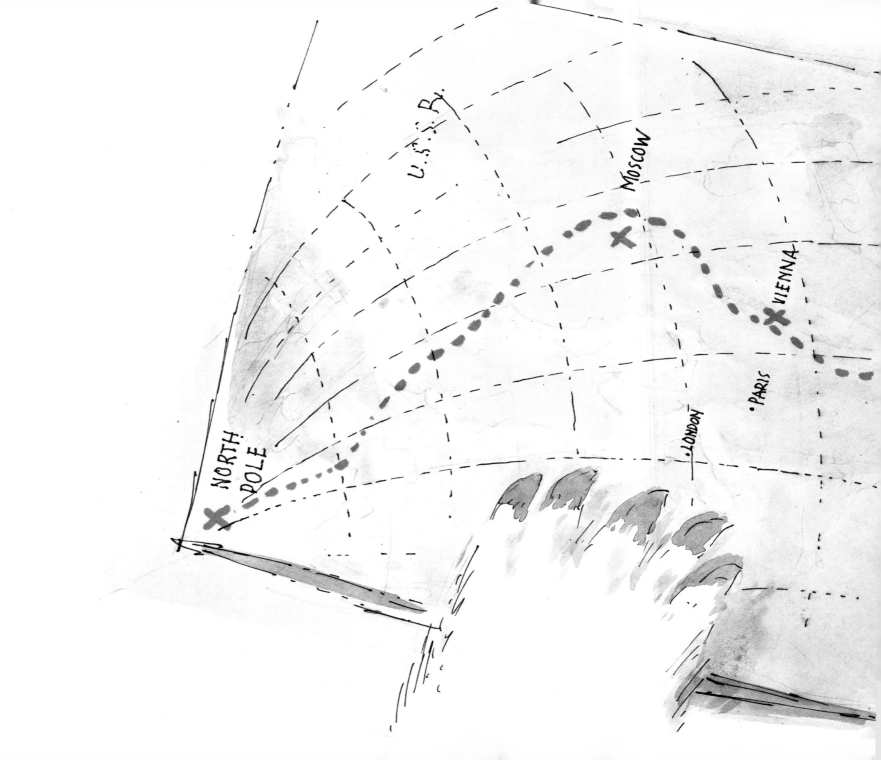

U.S.S.R.

MOSCOW

VIENNA

PARIS

LONDON

NORTH POLE

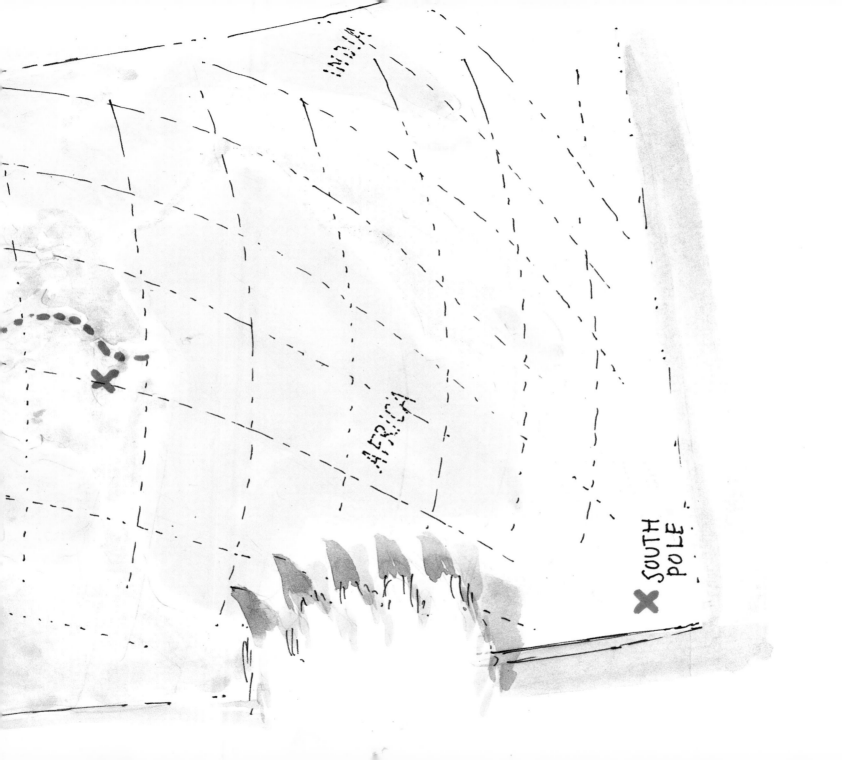

INDIA

AFRICA

SOUTH
POLE

'Why can't they feed cattle on fish?' he kept saying to himself crossly.

By the time the ship entered the harbour he had completely given up dreaming of Africa; all he thought about was fish. Even in his sleep he dreamed about fish and the more he slept the bigger and juicier the fish got.

The boat was unloaded in the daytime and despite the awful rumblings that his tummy made, Pushkin knew he would have to wait until nightfall before he could get out of the truck and begin his journey again. When the sun had finally fallen over the horizon, his stomach told him it was time to leave. Following his well-trained nose Pushkin was led to the old fish market by the docks. He sat down with lots of noisy cats who were there for the same purpose and began to feast on the left-over fish. Pushkin gorged himself until he nearly exploded. 'Oh, how good they taste,' he said to the cats as he ate his fourteenth fish.

The cats were fascinated by him. They sat and stared at this tubby white furry creature who ate more fish than all of them put together. When he had finished Pushkin concluded that boats were great fun only if you took your own supply of fish with you. With that thought he tied as many fish as he could to his scarf and set off into the night.

41

He wanted to get as far inland as he could before daybreak, for he did not like the thought of being caught and put in another zoo again. It was some time before he realized that Africa was one very large zoo without any walls. Working on the basis that rivers flow downhill, Pushkin followed the River Nile.

'Well, I'm going in the same direction,' he thought.

By dawn he came upon the Pyramids and the Sphynx. He could see no use for them at all. There were no roofs, and he couldn't find any doors or windows.

'What very strange people they must be who live here,' thought Pushkin, 'to build big useless things in the middle of nowhere.' (Pushkin was at times a very practical bear.) He didn't even bother to consider the Sphynx. Instead, he went for a swim in the Nile. It had been such a long time since he had swum, and the days were getting hotter and hotter. But his swim didn't last very long. A long, vicious, snarling animal chased him out of the water. Pushkin was not even sure if it was an animal. He was clever enough to see not only that it had far more teeth than he did, but obviously fancied him for breakfast. He did not stop to ask its name. 'There are many things that Digby did not tell me,' thought Pushkin as he lay drying in the sun.

For many days and nights Pushkin plodded through the Sahara Desert. After the first day he found it was easier to walk at night, when it was cooler. In the daytime he slept in what little shade he could find. Pushkin was luckier than most animals because his fur was white and did not attract the heat, but all the same it was fur. After his supply of fish had run out his longing to get home kept him going.

One day at dusk just as the sun was setting on the right-hand side of his map, he thought he saw trees in the distance. Pushkin had seen trees and water before, only to find out that they did not exist. Not too excited, he carried on in their direction. But this time they were real. He could not believe his luck, for it meant the end of the sand. So a very dirty and dusty Pushkin flopped into the pool of water. While he was splashing about and looking for fish he saw an orange streak whoosh past him.

'Hello,' shouted Pushkin. He had not seen an animal for many days and he had certainly never seen one that ran so fast. Unknown to Pushkin the orange streak had not seen a white furry creature before either. Carefully, the orange streak stopped. Pushkin thought he must not have heard his shout, so he carried on playing.

'Hello,' said the orange streak, taking Pushkin completely by surprise.

'Uhm hello,' said Pushkin, shaking himself as he climbed out of the pool.

'Who are you? I haven't met anyone like you before,' said the streak, still a little nervous of the rather plump white thing.

'My name is Pushkin. I'm a Polar Bear and . . . well, I'm going home.'

'I'm a cheetah, and I live around here. My name is Shaka.'

'Shaka, you run incredibly fast. How can you run that fast?' asked Pushkin wistfully, hoping that Shaka might teach him. 'If I could run as fast as Shaka I would be home in no time,' thought Pushkin. But he did not know that slightly fat Polar Bears are not built to run fast.

'It's quite simple really,' said Shaka. 'We cheetahs used to spend all our time lazing around in the sun, but the trouble was that most of the animals in the jungle were bigger than us and used to bully us, so we learnt to run very fast.' Shaka paused. 'We are not cowards you understand, it's just the way we learnt to survive.'

'Oh, I see,' said Pushkin, not really understanding at all. 'Please teach me to run like you,' he pleaded with eyes open and eager.

Shaka looked at Pushkin's legs and felt terribly sorry for him.

'That would be impossible, Pushkin. Look at my legs. They are long and thin and built for speed.'

Pushkin nodded.

'Look at yours. They are a bit short and fat, and not really built for running,' said Shaka with a sad look on his face. 'I'll tell you what I will do, though. I'll go and catch us some supper instead.'

'That's a good idea,' said Pushkin, who hadn't found any fish in the pool. Sad though he was that Shaka could not teach him to run quickly, he was very pleased at the idea of food.

They feasted themselves on meat, which Pushkin ate out of politeness. It was not as bad as the food they fed the cattle on, but nowhere nearly as nice as fish. Pushkin told Shaka all about his home and how he had met Digby. He even showed Shaka his map.

The next morning Pushkin left, waving goodbye to Shaka, who told him to try to stay in the open. Shaka wished him good luck, but did not promise to visit him. The cheetah did not like the sound of ice, snow and the cold. A few minutes later Pushkin came running back as fast as his little legs would carry him and told Shaka that he had seen an animal that was the same colour as Shaka. But it had a very long neck.

'What is it, Shaka? Will you grow up to be like that?' said Pushkin, still a little out of breath.

'No, Pushkin, that's a giraffe, totally different from me,' said Shaka giggling.

'How does he clean his ears?' said Pushkin, who was mystified by the strangest things.

Shaka roared with laughter and smiled at Pushkin. 'I have no idea how he cleans his ears, but don't worry, he won't harm you.'

Once again they said goodbye, and Pushkin went off on his journey. It wasn't long before he found a lake, a very big lake.

'Fish!' he shouted out as he dived in. That evening he cooked himself an enormous supper and went happily to sleep.

The next morning, just as he was beginning to wake up, he felt something poking his stomach.

'Who are you?' said a gruff voice.

'I could ask you the same,' said Pushkin in a dignified way. 'Do you always go around waking animals up when they are asleep? It's not very polite you know.' Pushkin was not always the best-mannered animal in the morning.

'What did you say?' said the gruff voice in disbelief.

'I asked you who you were, and what business you had waking me up,' said Pushkin, in a smaller voice.

The owner of the gruff voice was not only bigger than he was, but looked very angry indeed. 'I am a lion, and what's more I am the King of the Jungle.'

'Oh,' said Pushkin. 'Why are you the King of the Jungle?'

'What do you mean why? I just am,' said the lion, getting a little confused. Nobody had asked him before why he was the King of the Jungle.

'That is not a very good answer,' said Pushkin, inquisitive as ever.

'Well, I suppose I am the king because everybody is afraid of me,' said the lion.

'Oh, I see; you are the king because everybody is afraid of you, but that is not very fair.' Pushkin paused. 'What happens if someone else wants to be king?'

'Fair or not, I am the king, and come to think of it, no one has ever asked me before why I am the king.'

By this time the lion was totally confused, and forgot all about Pushkin, and went off muttering, 'Why am I king? Because I was born king. No, that cannot be right. There must be a reason.' Those were all the noises Pushkin could hear as he watched the lion walk away, scratching his head.

Pushkin felt very self-confident when he finally got up. 'I have talked to the King of the Jungle, and he did not attack me, so I doubt anyone else will,' he thought.

As the days went by, he saw many different animals, of all shapes and colours, and one day an elephant crashed out of the jungle with great thumping feet and offered to give him a ride. Pushkin gladly climbed on to the elephant's back and they lumbered off.

'This is a much more comfortable way to travel, and anyway, I'm too big to swing through the trees,' he thought as he watched the monkeys swinging above his head. Everything seemed to be going right at last. Riding on the elephant's back rested his sore feet, and he had even got used to the heat.

One lunch-time, when Pushkin was sitting down eating the fish from his scarf, he noticed an animal he had never seen before. It was playing in a waterfall, by a small lake. He decided to investigate, and do some fishing at the same time. The animal did not appear to notice Pushkin as it played happily in the lake. He stared until he plucked up enough courage to speak to it.

'Excuse me,' he said shyly, 'but what is your name?'

'I'm a unicorn, and I don't have a name,' said the beautiful pearl-coloured animal.

Pushkin was fascinated by the unicorn's one horn. 'I've heard of unicorns but – don't think I'm cheeky – I thought they did not exist,' said Pushkin, slightly bemused.

'Well aren't you talking to me?' said the unicorn.

'Yes,' said Pushkin positively.

'Then I exist, don't I?' Pushkin was a logical bear and could not find fault with the unicorn's reasoning.

'But why does everyone say there are no unicorns?' he asked.

'Many, many years ago, there was a flood, and all the world was covered in water. We unicorns are happy animals, and we did not want to stop playing when the rains fell. All the animals in the world were saved by a man named Noah, but the unicorns were drowned.'

Pushkin pretended to understand by nodding his head. 'Then you must be terribly old,' he said, still a little lost for words, but trying to be logical.

'I am,' said the unicorn, who paused, and then said, 'your name is Pushkin, isn't it?'

'How did you know that?' asked Pushkin in amazement.

'When you are as old as I am, there are very few things you do not know. Now listen carefully, Pushkin. You believe you are talking to me, don't you?' Pushkin nodded his head.

'And you believe that you will get home.' Again Pushkin nodded his head.

'Then maybe that is why we met, and why I know your name.'

Before Pushkin could say anything the beautiful unicorn vanished. He just disappeared through the waterfall.

Very soon, almost as if someone was showing him the way Pushkin found the sea that Digby had marked on the map. Polar Bears are very good swimmers, so he dived straight into the cold green water. For a long time Pushkin swam and caught fish at the same time. It was like paradise after the hot journey. He had learnt to sleep in the water by lying on his back and floating.

'This is much better than the desert,' he thought.

It wasn't long before he saw on the horizon small white mountains that he knew were near home. He scrambled on to the first iceberg and jumped up and down many times shouting, 'I'm home, I'm home.'

He recognized the coast and he knew he did not have far to go. If he hurried he would be with his mother and father before nightfall. His nose led him straight there.

'Hello,' said Pushkin, as he went through the opening of his home.

'Pushkin, is that you?' called his mother.

'Yes, of course.'

'Where have you been?' she said in an angry voice.

'First of all . . .'

His mother interrupted him. 'Just look at the state of your paws; now go and clean them at once.'

'But, I was telling . . .' started poor Pushkin eagerly.

'Go and do as you are told,' said his mother.

'What a strange welcome after all this time; not even the lion talked to me like that,' thought Pushkin unhappily.

'If you don't hurry up, there will be no supper for you. You're late again and you look an absolute mess.'

'So would you if you had walked half-way across the world,' said Pushkin.

'Don't be cheeky, Pushkin,' said his father in a quiet voice. 'Now go and do what your mother told you.'

Muttering to himself, Pushkin went off to clean his paws. 'What do they know? I escape from a zoo, walk across the world and all they are worried about is the state of my paws,' thought Pushkin.

Having washed his paws, he went down to supper.

'Now, Pushkin, where have you been? Your mother and I have been very worried,' said his father.

'Well,' said Pushkin rubbing his tummy, 'that's a long story.'